Section 2 **Court case**

5 John's defence lawyer told the court
   a he had never driven a car before.
   b he should be acquitted because he was innocent.
   c he wasn't driving the car illegally.
   d he only broke the law because of the special circumstances.

6 The prosecution stated that
   a John wasn't capable of driving a car.
   b the public had to be protected from young drivers.
   c John had broken the law and his reasons were no excuse.
   d John should be severely punished for not taking the test.

Listen to the conversation again and write down the answers to these questions.

7 Find a word or phrase on the tape which means the same as these:
   a remember

   ....

   b about to, on the point of

   ....

   c allowed, permitted

   ....

   d a (heart) illness

   ....

   e excitedly, in a panic

   ....

   f very fast

   ....

   g careless, irresponsible

   ....

   h a person who obeys the law

   ....

   i undesirable, unpleasant

   ....

Unit 3 Crime and the law

8 Listen for the three ways 'I should say' is pronounced in the dialogue and write down the different meaning on each occasion.

a ....

b ....

....

c ....

....

9 Complete these conditional sentences.
  a John would never have taken the car if

....

....

  b If John's mother hadn't received the tablets in time

....

FOLLOW-UP
In groups or pairs, discuss what punishment you would give to John if you were the magistrate. Then discuss how your decision would alter if John had had an accident and injured someone while driving the car.

Section 3 **Burglaries**

VOCABULARY
Burglary (noun) a robbery where a person breaks into a house to steal
Burglar (noun) person who does as above (**to burgle** (verb))
Appalling (adj.) shocking or terrible
Outlay (noun) expense
Bolt (noun) a kind of lock on a door
To be wary (phrase) to be cautious or suspicious
Credentials (noun) papers or documents giving the holder's identity
Opportunist (noun) person who takes advantage of a situation for his/her own ends

Section 3 **Burglaries**

Superintendent Norman Parker of Scotland Yard is giving a lecture on crime. In this excerpt he is giving some hints about how to avoid having your house burgled.
  Listen to the first part of the lecture, which is reproduced below, and fill in the missing figures, numbers and words.

A house is burgled in Britain now about every ....

and over the past .... the
number of burglaries reported to the police has risen by approximately

.................., to well over .... this year. The insurance companies report that last year alone household burglary losses rose by

.... over the previous year to ...., and I believe

.... or .... companies are refusing to provide cover in what we might call high-risk areas.

Listen to the rest of the lecture and fill in the tables. One example is already given.

Things you should do to avoid a burglary

---

1 Fit good locks and bolts on doors and windows.

Unit 3 **Crime and the law**

Things you should not do to avoid a burglary

FOLLOW-UP
Write a dialogue between a householder and a salesman selling burglar alarms.

Unit 4 **Jobs**

Section 1 **Getting a job**

VOCABULARY
To scour (verb) to examine carefully
Curriculum vitae (Latin phrase) a brief account of one's education, employment and so on (often abbreviated to **c.v.**)
Crammed full (adj. phrase) full of
Graduate (noun) a person who has a university degree
A crash course (idiomatic phrase) an intensive course
Slick (adj.) smooth, efficient
Legible (adj.) readable
Blot, stain (nouns) dirty mark
Short list (noun) a final list of the best applications for a job, containing people to be interviewed

In the tape, a radio reporter examines some of the difficulties involved in getting a job. Now listen to the tape and answer the following questions.

1 What does the book *Getting a Job* contain?

   ....

   ....

2 What two kinds of mistakes does Judith Davidson say an application form or c.v. often contains?

   a ....

   b ....

3 Listen for the word or phrase which means
   a inarticulate

   ....

   b clumsy

   ....

4 What do students learn at the training college?

   ....

   ....

37

Unit 4 **Jobs**

5 Write down five things mentioned by Judith Davidson which are wrong with letters of application.

a ....

b ....

c ....

d ....

e ....

6 Tick [✓] the statements in the table below about Mark Ashworth which are true.

a Mark Ashworth thinks a good application will get you a job.	
b Mark Ashworth works full time writing c.v.s for others.	
c Mark Ashworth has a business in the USA.	
d Mark Ashworth has only written 250 c.v.s.	
e Mark Ashworth thinks that 80 per cent of job applications are inadequate.	

7 What mistakes does Mark Ashworth think people make with c.v.s?

a ....

b ....

c ....

d ....
....

e ....

Section 2 **Interviews**

8 What does Mark try to achieve in the interview with his clients?

   ....

   ....

9 What are three essential elements of handwritten applications?

   a ....

   b ....

   c ....

10 Tick [√] the statements in the table below about Judith Davidson which are true.

a She believes all applicants are judged by their handwriting.	
b She thinks people often forget vital things.	
c She says people should send a letter with their application.	
d She says personal details can be useful.	
e She says an employer will see between two and three hundred people.	

Section 2 **Interviews**

VOCABULARY
Hurdle (figurative noun) a difficulty to be overcome
To dread (verb) to be afraid of
To falter (verb) to speak hesitantly or nervously
To stammer (verb) to speak hesitantly or nervously
Ogre (noun) a frightening person
To squirm (verb) to fidget nervously
To twiddle (verb) to twist or play with something nervously
Frumpy (adj.) dressed in old-fashioned clothes
Laid-back (colloquial adj.) very relaxed, very casual

Unit 4 **Jobs**

Mr Robert Tunbridge is the Director of the Central Employment Agency. He is talking to a group of young people about job interviews.
  Now listen to the tape and answer these questions:
1 What things does Robert Tunbridge want to show his listeners?

   a ....

   ....

   b ....

   c ....

   ....

2 What's the screening interview for?

   ....

   ....

3 In the table below, tick [✓] the statements about Anita Jones which are true.

a She grew up in Southampton.	
b Her father works in a bank.	
c She has only worked occasionally before.	
d She was only attracted to the job because of the money.	

4 Fill in below some of the mistakes which Anita made in her interview. One has been done for you as an example.

   a She was very nervous.

   b ....

   c ....

   d ....

   e ....

   f ....

Section 2 **Interviews**

g ....

5 From the interview with Louise Simpson, write down:
  a When will the new building be finished?

  ....

  b What did she read about in the prospectus?

  ....

  c Why did she work in the lawyer's office?

  ....

  d What benefit did she get from working there?

  ....

6 Fill in below the things which Robert Tunbridge tells his listeners they should do at a job interview.

  a ....

  b ....

  c ....

  d ....

  e ....

  f ....

  g ....

  h ....

FOLLOW-UP

As a role-play exercise, work in groups and make up some advertisements for jobs. Then give them to the other groups so they can apply for the jobs. Then act out the subsequent interviews, taking the parts of interviewer and applicant. Afterwards, comment on each other's performance.

Unit 4 **Jobs**

Section 3 **Phone-in**

VOCABULARY
On the job (idiomatic phrase) while at work
Flautist (noun) flute-player
Aggro (colloquial noun) anger, discord (short for: aggravation)
To glower (verb) to look angrily at someone
Without batting an eyelid (idiomatic phrase) without getting excited or showing any emotion
Woodwind (noun) wind instruments in an orchestra
Plumber (noun) worker who fits and repairs water pipes
To trek (verb) to walk a long way
Anecdote (noun) short amusing story
To writhe (verb) to twist or roll about

Now listen to the tape and answer the questions below. You will hear an excerpt from a radio programme in which several people phone in to talk about strange or funny experiences they've had at work. The questions are divided up according to the people who telephone.

1 The bassoon player
Tick [✓] the statements which are true in the table below.

a Paul always listens to Helen's programme.	
b The flute section was in front of Paul.	
c Sonia was jealous of Arthur.	
d Sonia had less experience than Arthur.	
e Sonia couldn't play because she was chewing gum.	
f Arthur didn't show he was amused by Sonia's problem.	
g Sonia tore up her music in anger.	

2 The chambermaid
   a Explain the meaning of the phrase 'you've worked your way up the ladder'.

   ....

   ....

Section 3 **Phone-in**

   b Why would Lucy's story be hard for anyone from a hot country to believe?

   ....

   ....

   c What was the attraction of the place she was working in?

   ....

   ....

   d Listen for the phrase which means 'the boiler stopped working'.

   ....

   ....

   e What had happened in the night?

   ....

   ....

3 Spiders
   a Why was Professor St Clair in Thailand?

   ....

   ....

   b Who was with the professor?

   ....

   ....

   c What is arachnology?

   ....

   ....

   d What is the meaning of the phrase 'out of shouting range'?

   ....

   ....

Unit 4 **Jobs**

    e Concerning the handkerchief:
        i Why was the colour special?

        ....

        ii Why was it on the ground?

        ....

    f Listen for the word or phrase the professor uses to say how upset he was over what had happened.

        ....

        ....

4 Computers

    a Why was Wilma Sutherland in a hurry?

        ....

    b What do these expressions mean?
        i To grab a bite

        ....

        ii Whatever was handy

        ....

        iii A string of four-letter words

        ....

        iv To mop it up

        ....

        ....

Section 3 **Phone-in**

   c What two reasons are given for the computer not working after the incident?

      i ....

      ii ....

5 The fireman
  a Why else are firemen called out, apart from to put out fires?

      i ....

      ii ....

  b Why couldn't the fireman see in the bathroom?

     ....

     ....

  c Why was the policeman not afraid of going into the bathroom?

     ....

     ....

  d **i** What was in the bathroom?

     ....

       ii Why?

     ....

     ....

     ....

FOLLOW-UP

In groups, make up your own radio phone-in programme and record it on tape, if possible. Nominate one member of the group as the announcer and then recount some experiences you yourselves have had which are strange or funny. When you have made your tape, play it to the other groups in the class.

Unit 5 **Sport**

Section 1 **Round-up**

VOCABULARY
A round-up (noun) a summary
To deter (verb) to put off
Relegation (noun) to be moved down to a lower level
Draw (noun) match where the score is equal on both sides
Hassle (colloquial noun) fuss, bother, trouble
To call it a day (idiomatic phrase) to decide something is finished, over
Outsider (noun) when used in connection with sport, this means someone not considered to have a chance of winning

At the end of a news bulletin Mike Ross, a television sports commentator, is giving details of the main sporting events of the day.
 Listen to the tape and write down the answers to these questions, which have been divided into sections according to the sports referred to.

Football
1 What might have made fans not want to go to the match?

   ....

   ....
2 What was the score?

   ....
3 When did Dennis Bridge score his goal?

   ....
4 Who scored the second goal?

   ....
5 Why did Leeds United want to win this match?

   ....

   ....
6 a How much did Leeds United pay for Tom Wallace?

   ....

   b What team did he play for previously?

   ....

Section 1 **Round-up**

7 What was the score in the Queens Park Rangers v. Southampton match?

   ....

Tennis
8 Where is Veronica Potter ranked

   a in Britain? ....

   b in the world? ....
9 What was the score in each of the three sets of the match between Veronica Potter and Tina Morris?

   ....

10 What is John Barclay doing next month?

   ....

   ....

Athletics
11 In the table, beside the names of the competitors mentioned, fill in their country, the event they took part in and their place in the event. Some have already been done for you.

Name	Country	Event	Place
a Christina Krämer			1st
b Tanya Lyubimova	USSR	Women's 100m	
c Lorraine Garland			
d Janet Carter	Britain		
e Trevor Smith			1st

47

Unit 5 **Sport**

Name	Country	Event	Place
f Steve Petts			
g Wolf Rainer		Men's 1500m	
h Angelo Pirelli			
i Tom Oakes			
j Pierre Maurier		Long jump	
k Lek Cusmir			

Golf
12 In last year's US Golf Championships

   a who won? ....

   b who was second? ....

13 Who's playing Manuel Garcia tomorrow?

   ....

Football results
14 Now fill in the table below about the football results given.

Division	Team	Result	Team	Result
a 1	Arsenal			0
b			Everton	
c		3		
d	Fulham			

Section 2 **Olympics**

FOLLOW-UP

In groups or pairs, study the sports pages of a newspaper and write your own sports round-up using the information given. Then record it on a cassette and play it to the rest of the class. If you wish, you can even make up your own questions about it.

Section 2 **Olympics**

VOCABULARY

Agenda (noun) a list of the subjects discussed at a meeting
Minutes (noun) notes written down about a previous meeting
To sound out opinion (idiomatic phrase) to find out the general opinion
To uphold (verb) to support or maintain (standards)
To detract from (verb) to take away the credit
Arbitrarily (adv.) thoughtlessly, without considering the wishes of others
Fencing (noun) the sport of fighting with swords
Archery (noun) the sport of shooting with bows and arrows
Equestrian (adj.) used to describe sports involving horseriding
Canoeing (noun) sport in which a light boat is moved by one or more paddles
To axe (verb) to cut out, remove

In this discussion the Policy Committee of the Olympic Council are discussing a proposal which has been put before them. Those taking part in the discussion are: Mr Henry Carter from Australia (the Chairman), Mrs Martha Armstrong from Canada, Herr Werner Müller from Austria, Sr Fernando Cordoba from Peru and Mrs Indira Patel from India.

Now listen to the tape and write down the answers to these questions.
1 What is the proposal before the Committee?

   ....

   ....

2 Give the three reasons why Mrs Armstrong doesn't want to reduce the size of the Olympic Games.

   a ....

   b ....

   c ....

Unit 5 **Sport**

3 During the course of the discussion the members of the Committee mention the names of several sports and give various reasons why they should be excluded from the Olympic Games. Fill in the table below, giving the name of the speaker, the sport mentioned and his or her reasons for leaving it out of the Olympic programme. The first one has been done for you as an example.

Name of speaker	Sport mentioned	Reason for exclusion
a Sr Cordoba	Boxing	The lobby against its violent nature
b		
c		
d		
e		
f		

Section 2 **Olympics**

4 Which of these words best describes the attitude of the members of the Committee to the proposal? Match the word to the name.

    Mrs Armstrong   constructive
    Herr Müller   conciliatory
    Sr Cordoba   totally opposed
    Mrs Patel   favourable

5 At the end of the discussion, the Chairman briefly summarises the opinions given in the meeting. Make notes on what he says and then in your own words outline the arguments put forward. You will need about 75 words.

....
....
....
....
....
....
....
....
....
....
....
....

6 Now listen to the discussion again and write down the words and phrases you hear which are used
   a by the Chairman to start the meeting officially.

....
....

Unit 5 **Sport**

b by Mrs Armstrong to disagree with the proposal.

....

....

c by Herr Müller to tell Mrs Armstrong that they can all understand her point of view.

....

....

d by Sr Cordoba to say that he is unwilling to change the Games.

....

....

e by Mrs Patel to say that she completely agrees with what has just been said.

....

....

f by the Chairman to tell the members not to lose their tempers.

....

....

FOLLOW-UP

In groups, discuss

a whether you think team sports are more enjoyable than individual sports.
b whether you think big international sports competitions like the Olympic Games promote international understanding.

Then compare your ideas with those of the other groups.

Section 3 **Sport in Britain**

VOCABULARY
Recreation (noun) exercise
Affiliated (adj.) associated, connected
To cater for (verb) to satisfy the needs of
Solely (adv.) only

The tape contains an excerpt from a lecture on sport in Britain given by a junior Sports Minister. Listen to it and answer the questions below.

1 What sport is connected with these three places?

   a Wembley ....

   b Murrayfield ....

   c Wimbledon ....

2 Name four sports or other leisure activities mentioned which have become increasingly popular.

   a ....

   b ....

   c ....

   d ....

   ....

3 Several figures are given on the tape by the speaker, some of which are reproduced below. Write down what each one refers to. The first one has been done for you as an example.
   a   19   The nineteenth century, when football began.

   b   400   ....

   c   92   ....

   d   4   ....

   e   3   ....

Unit 5 **Sport**

    f 27 million ....

    g £500m ....

4 How many kilometres of waterways does the British Waterways Board maintain? Circle the correct answer.
    a 1760
    b 2720
    c 960

5 Other than using local authority facilities, where else can adults practise sport?

    a ....

    b ....

6 Give three amenities, other than playing fields, which exist at different schools.

    a ....

    b ....

    c ....

7 What are the 'centres of sporting excellence'?

....

....

FOLLOW-UP
In groups or pairs, imagine you are a local authority responsible for providing sports facilities for your community. As you have a limited budget, decide which of the items listed below you will spend your money on. You may choose only six.

golf course	football ground
swimming pool	riding club
tennis courts	rowing club
athletics track	artificial ski slope
bowling alley	badminton courts
squash courts	gymnasium

Unit 6 **Technology**

Section 1 **Cross-Channel power**

Part A **The project**

VOCABULARY
To kick off (verb) to begin, start
To go (according) to plan (idiomatic phrase) to proceed as planned
To swap (verb) to exchange
To do your own thing (idiomatic phrase) to act independently
Barge (noun) a large flat-bottomed boat
Drawback (noun) disadvantage
Shell (noun) a the hard outer covering of some sea animals
  b a metal case filled with explosive which is fired from a gun
To pose problems (idiomatic phrase) to present difficulties
To fill someone in (verb) to give information

Listen to the conversation about the joint French–British project to lay electricity cables across the Channel. Pamela Hargreaves is interviewing two engineers from the project – Mark Fraser from the CEGB (Central Electricity Generating Board) in Britain and Christophe Plisson from Électricité de France.

1 Fill in the following information:

a starting date ....

b completion date ....

c planning time ....

d number of cables ....

e length ....

f cost ....

g output ....

h problems i ....

    ii ....

    iii ....

55

Unit 6 **Technology**

2 Fill in the information about the two machines:

	French	British
a Name		
b Weight		
c Description		
d Guided or controlled by		
e Advantages	i ii	
f Disadvantages		

Section 1 **Cross-Channel power**

3 Fill in the names on the map.

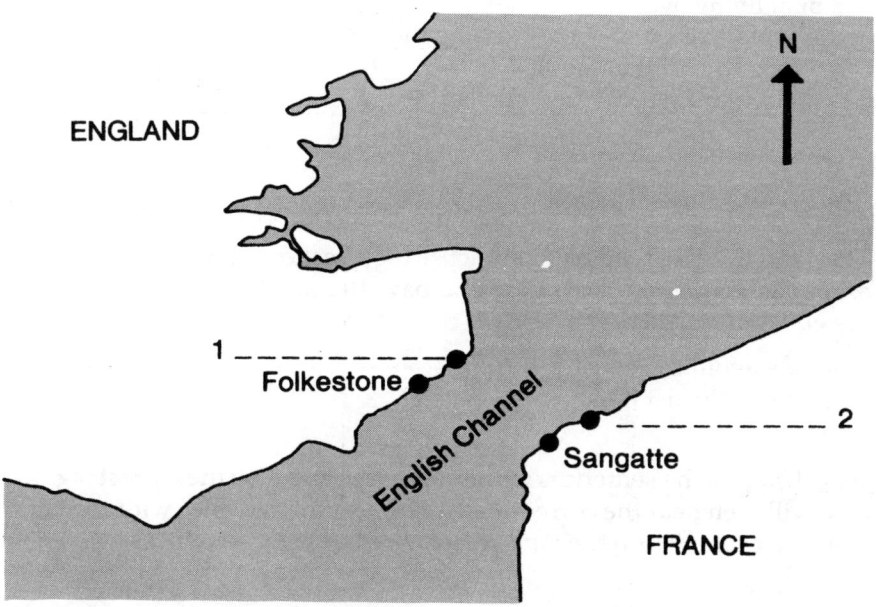

Listen to the discussion again and choose the correct answer. Put a circle around **a** or **b** to indicate your choice.

1 The planning took **a** more time than laying the cable.
　　　　　　　　　　b less
2 There are **a** four cables.
　　　　　　b eight
3 Folkestone is **a** far from Dover.
　　　　　　　　b near
4 French power is **a** less expensive than British power.
　　　　　　　　　b more
5 The RTM III is **a** a little heavier than the French digger.
　　　　　　　　　b a lot
6 The **a** French machine is better for hard rock.
　　　　b British

FOLLOW-UP

In two groups, prepare a radio or television interview with people who are involved with this project. One group will be reporters or journalists and the other group will be the different individuals. Some examples of people to interview are:

a a French diver
b a crew member on the barge

57

Unit 6 **Technology**

c a repairman for the RTM III
d a pilot flying over
e the captain of a ferry boat crossing the Channel
f a repairman for the Limule I
g a resident from Sangatte or Folkestone

Part B **Tag questions**

This is an exercise to help you practise tag questions. Listen to the examples from the conversation and pay attention to the use of tags at the end of the sentences. Here are the first two.

It took about three years, *didn't it*?
It's basically just huge cables, *isn't it*?

Now listen to the sentences without the tags and give the correct tag. You will then hear the correct answer; repeat the sentence with the tag. The two examples on the tape are followed by eight sentences.

Section 2 **Tiny TVs**

VOCABULARY
To up the production (idiomatic phrase) to increase
To pull out all the stops (idiomatic phrase) to do everything possible
To design from scratch (idiomatic phrase) to plan something from the beginning
To take off (verb) to increase quickly
To unveil (a product) (verb) to show it for the first time
To jump on the bandwagon (idiomatic phrase) to take advantage of the success of something
To back a winner (idiomatic phrase) to support something that is successful
To keep in touch with something (idiomatic phrase) to maintain contact

Fred Fletcher, a BBC reporter, is talking to Vic Robinson about the increasing popularity of very small televisions. Listen to the conversation and fill in the details in the table.

Section 2 **Tiny TVs**

| Company | Production | | Description |
	Year	Number	
1 Japan **a** Sony	i ii Spring 1983		
b			
c		2000 per month	
2 Britain	1983		

59

Unit 6 **Technology**

Listen to the conversation again and choose the correct answers to the following. Put a circle around **a, b, c** or **d** to indicate your choice.

1 The market for tiny televisions
   a is getting smaller every year.
   b is increasing rapidly.
   c is expanding only in Japan.
   d began in the seventies.

2 The new model of the Watchman was launched
   a six months ago.
   b when production reached 2000 units per month.
   c two years after the first model.
   d one year after the first model.

3 With the Hattori model
   a the TV screen is part of the battery pack.
   b the headphones are connected to the TV screen.
   c the TV receiver is connected to the watch.
   d the battery is built into the watch.

4 The Sinclair model is
   a similar in size to the Sony.
   b similar in size to the Casio.
   c only a novelty item.
   d 20 per cent smaller than the Sony.

5 The main market that the companies are aiming at is people who
   a work on trains and buses.
   b like novelty items.
   c have monotonous work.
   d travel on trains and buses.

FOLLOW-UP

1 In small groups, plan an advertising campaign for small televisions aimed at the following markets:

   a teenagers
   b commuters
   c executives
   d housewives
   e college students
   f pensioners

Section 3 **Hot off the press**

2 In pairs, prepare a dialogue between a shop assistant and a customer wanting to buy a small television for:
   a a Christmas present for Grandmother
   b a birthday gift for a teenager
   c a prize for a factory competition
   d a friend in hospital
   e a retirement gift

Section 3 **Hot off the press**

VOCABULARY
Bits and pieces (idiomatic phrase) small things, little pieces of information
Titbit (noun) an interesting, attractive bit
To stuff (verb) to push tightly into something
PVC plastic polyvinyl chloride plastic
RAM (computer term) random access memory
Odds and ends (idiomatic phrase) little bits of things, small items

1 Listen to the details of the recent developments in the field of science and technology. Pay special attention to names and numbers and then fill in the notes for each reference.

   a Alpha   Name of microrobot

   b 30   Height (cm) of Alpha

   c 1666   ....

   d 80   ....

   e Taiwan   ....

   f LCD   ....

   g 8   ....

   h STP   ....

   i 26,000   ....

   j 350 million   ....

Unit 6 **Technology**

2 Listen to the information again and, with the help of your notes, write questions for the following answers. They are not in the same order as on the tape.

Question	Answer
a How much does the STP weigh?	a 26,000 tonnes
b Which company made the watch with the recording device?	b Seiko
c	c Alaska
d	d 700 g
e	e PVC
f	f 1455
g	g Flex-O-Calc
h	h California
i	i South Korea
j	j 30 minutes

Section 3 **Hot off the press**

FOLLOW-UP

1 In pairs, practise describing precise processes and choose one of the following:

   a How a robot arm can put a sheet of paper into a box.
   b How to set a digital watch to wake you up at 0615.
   c How to set a radio-cassette recorder to record the news on the radio.
   d How to make a pot of tea or coffee.
   e How to change the refill in a ball-point pen.
   f How to change the batteries in a tape recorder.
   g How to use a pocket calculator.

2 In small groups, prepare news items about the following:

   a A solar-powered watch.
   b A bridge to connect Britain and France.
   c A mini microrobot.
   d The smallest TV in the world.
   e The largest cinema screen in the world.
   f A revolutionary new pocket calculator.
   g The largest oil rig in the world.

Unit 7 Fashion

Section 1 Psychology of clothes

VOCABULARY
Prospective (adj.) expected, hoped for, intended
The conscious mind (noun) the part of the mind which is awake, able to understand what is happening
The subconscious mind (noun) the part of the mind which operates at a hidden level
Homesick (adj.) sad because you are away from home
Outgoing (adj.) extrovert, friendly
Sociable (adj.) friendly, talkative
(It) speaks volumes about (idiomatic phrase) it tells a lot about, gives a lot of information about
To rebel (verb) to disagree with authority or fixed standards
Rebelliousness (noun) disagreeing with authority
(He's) pushing middle age (idiomatic phrase) he's approaching middle age
(I) go along wholeheartedly with it (idiomatic phrase) I agree with it absolutely

Pauline Sheldon, the Fashion Editor of the *Daily News*, is being interviewed by Janice Waring. In this excerpt she is talking about the effect clothes have on other people. Listen to the tape and then answer the questions.

1 What has Pauline Sheldon just said before the excerpt begins?

....

....

2 What two things govern the clothes we wear?

a ....

b ....

3 What two things might wearing warm clothes indicate?

a ....

b ....

4 What part does colour play, according to Pauline?

....

....

Section 1 **Psychology of clothes**

5 What two things are said about trousers and what do they mean?

a ....

....

b ....

....

6 What does wearing unconventional clothes mean, according to Pauline?

....

....

7 Give three aspects of personality that can be conveyed by clothes.

a ....

b ....

c ....

8 a What kind of clothes do employers like executives to wear?

....

b Why?

....

9 What is Pauline Sheldon's opinion about wearing sober clothes?

....

....

....

FOLLOW-UP
In groups or pairs:
1 Decide what clothes you would wear to

a a wedding.   b a job interview.   c a party.

2 Discuss whether the clothes we wear say anything about our character. Give specific examples from your own experience.
3 Discuss what changes have taken place in fashions over the past few years and try to predict new fashions of the future.

Unit 7 **Fashion**

Section 2 **Fashion model**

VOCABULARY
Glossy magazines (noun) high-quality fashion magazines
To delve into (verb) to investigate, look into
Freelance (adj.) working for yourself and not a company
Poise (noun) the way in which one carries oneself
To pack in (colloquial verb) to give up
Cosseted (adj.) looked after very well, fussed over
Hectic (adj.) very excited, feverish
To cart around (colloquial verb) to carry around

Now listen to the tape about a fashion model and answer these questions.

1 How can a model earn as much as a top secretary?

   ....

   ....

2 Describe briefly what the Metropolitan Academy of Modelling does.

   ....

   ....

3 How old is Margaret Connor now?

   ....

4 Name three things you can learn at the Academy.

   a ....

   b ....

   c ....

5 Describe Margaret Connor.

   ....

   ....

6 What can we tell from her photograph?

   ....

   ....

Section 2 **Fashion model**

7 Give three reasons why Denise Harper chose Margaret Connor for the course – because she had:

   a ....

   b ....

   c ....

8 Why do some girls give up modelling? Because:

   a ....

   b ....

   c ....

9 What have you got to do to succeed in modelling?

....

10 Briefly outline the differences in the kinds of days described.

   a ....
   ....

   b ....
   ....

11 Why are TV commercials more fun to make?

....
....

12 Explain these two phrases.
   a 'Every model has one arm longer than the other.'

   ....
   ....

   b 'Everything but the kitchen sink.'

   ....
   ....

Unit 7 **Fashion**

13 Why does Margaret Connor like her work so much?

   ....

   ....

14 In this tape the interviewer does not pose the questions directly to the interviewees. Listen to the whole tape again and make notes so that you can compose the questions he might have asked to produce the answers given by Margaret Connor and Denise Harper. The first two here have been done for you as examples.

   a How much can an average model earn?

   b What can you learn at a modelling academy?

   c ....

   ....

   d ....

   ....

   ....

   e ....

   ....

   f ....

   ....

   g ....

   ....

   h ....

FOLLOW-UP

In groups or pairs:
1 Discuss what kind of person makes a good model.
2 Discuss the advantages and disadvantages of the life of a model.
3 Prepare an advertisement for a new line of sports clothes and then present it to the other students.

Section 3 **Fashion notebook**

VOCABULARY
Haute couture (French term) high fashion
Chunk (noun) a piece
Slant (noun) inclination, point of view
Stunning (adj.) amazing, exciting
Craft (noun) skill, work
To buy in bulk (verb phrase) to buy in large quantities
Venue (noun) location, place

Selina Simmons, a radio fashion correspondent, is giving details of the latest developments in fashion. In her talk she concentrates on three separate items, and the questions have been divided accordingly.
  Now listen to the tape and answer the questions.

1

What do Edinburgh and Tokyo have in common?	
What is Whitmore's?	
Who buys many of Tom Pickford's Scottish fabrics?	
When was the last fashion show at the Dorset Hotel?	
What does Kenko design?	
What is the connection between Yoshi Tamura and Paris?	
What does Tom Pickford get from his fashion shows?	
What accounts for 20 per cent of Whitmore's sales?	

Unit 7 **Fashion**

Now answer these questions about fashion in Spain by circling **a, b, c** or **d** to indicate your choice.

2 When Selina Simmons mentions landing at a Spanish airport, she is really saying that
   a the authorities often lose your luggage in transit.
   b to lose your luggage would give you a chance to replace it with good Spanish clothes.
   c it would be very unlucky if you lost all your luggage in Spain.
   d it would be better not to take any luggage with you when you go to Spain in case you lose it.

3 Referring to Spanish clothes, Selina says
   a that there is a good new variety of clothes available in Spain.
   b that the new fashions in Spain will mean that everybody has to get a new wardrobe.
   c new clothes in Spain are designed very quickly.
   d that it is a lot of trouble to buy clothes in Spain.

4 Evening wear in Spain
   a has been copied from original Japanese designs.
   b is imported from Spain by Japanese designers.
   c has been influenced quite a lot by Japanese designers.
   d is made by Japanese designers living in Spain.

5 Selina says that Spanish designers
   a are much better than famous French ones.
   b are not as good as French ones.
   c only design clothes suitable for the cold weather.
   d may soon threaten other international designers.

6 Fashion goods from Spain
   a sell well all over the world.
   b are popular in the Middle East and Scandinavia.
   c are mostly made of leather.
   d are now sold widely in Britain.

Section 3 **Fashion notebook**

Now answer these questions about the last part of Selina's talk.

7 Mark the statements below with a T for True or an F for False.

a A home dressmaker has difficulty finding good fabrics.	
b A home dressmaker needs good fabric.	
c A home dressmaker has to buy fabric in large quantities.	
d A home dressmaker should only buy surplus material.	
e A home dressmaker could benefit from Mike Hastings' sales.	

8 If the date of the next sale in Bath is Thursday, 10 October, fill in the table below.

Place	Date of sale
a	Thursday, 3 October
b Bath	Thursday, 10 October
c	
d Southampton	
e Norwich	

9 If I lived in Manchester, what number should I ring to get details of the sales?

....

Unit 8 **Environment and ecology**

Section 1 **Volcanoes**

Part A **Mt Etna**

VOCABULARY
To erupt (verb) to explode and pour out fire (for volcanoes)
To blast (verb) to blow up, usually with explosives
To detonate (a charge) (verb) to explode suddenly, often with a loud noise
Lava (noun) the hot liquid rock flowing from a volcano
To have something up your sleeve (idiomatic phrase) to have a surprise in store

An Italian reporter from Mt Etna in Sicily is giving some information about the mountain and the eruption. Listen to the report and make notes. Then listen again and choose the correct answer for the following statements. Put a circle around **a, b, c** or **d** to indicate your choice.

1 The reporter is standing
   a at the bottom of the mountain.
   b at the edge of the lava flow.
   c on the old lava wall.
   d at none of the above.

2 The volcano
   a is about to erupt.
   b has finished erupting.
   c is still erupting.
   d hasn't erupted for more than twenty years.

3 Etna is
   a the highest mountain in Europe.
   b the most active volcano in Europe.
   c the highest active volcano in Europe.
   d none of the above.

4 It has erupted just over twenty times
   a since 1669.
   b since the first eruption.
   c in the past 75 years.
   d none of the above.

5 The lava is flowing
   a diagonally eastwards.
   b directly eastwards.

Section 1 **Volcanoes**

    c westwards.
    d southwards.

6 Houses are being built
    a near the old lava wall.
    b at the bottom of the mountain.
    c close to the flow of lava.
    d at none of the above.

7 Listen to the tape again and look at the following True/False sentences. Mark T for True and F for False.

a The lava is coming out of an opening at the top of the mountain.	
b Lava moves more quickly when it's cool.	
c Concrete is a greater threat than lava, according to one expert.	
d Mt Etna erupts at regular intervals.	
e Mt Etna has erupted more often in the twentieth century than in previous centuries.	

8 This exercise concentrates on numbers and figures. Write questions using the introductory word *how* for the following answers. Here is an example to show you:

	Question	*Answer*
a	How high is Mt Etna?	a 3200 m
b	....	b 39
c	....	c 22
d	....	d 1 million m^3

73

Unit 8 **Environment and ecology**

e .... e 2300 m

f .... f a dozen

....

g .... g millions of pounds

....

h .... h 100 m

i .... i 500 kg

FOLLOW-UP
In two groups, prepare interviews with people about the eruption of Mt Etna. One group will be reporters or journalists and the other group will be different individuals. Some examples of people to interview are:

a a tourist from Denmark
b a French volcanologist
c the owner of a tourist shop near Mt Etna
d one of the engineers
e a BBC documentary photographer
f the president of the local environment group
g the manager of the construction company which is building villas near the bottom of the mountain
h a local resident
i a woman whose house was destroyed in the previous eruption

Part B Krakatoa

VOCABULARY
Repercussion (noun) far-reaching and indirect effect
Death toll (noun) number of deaths
Tidal wave (noun) great ocean wave, often destructive
Algae (noun) simple water plants
Fern (noun) feathery, green-leaved flowerless plant
Teak (noun) tall evergreen tree in India, Malaysia, Burma
Mahogany (noun) tropical tree with dark brown wood
To obliterate (verb) to destroy, to remove all signs of

Section 1 **Volcanoes**

Listen to this account about the eruption of the volcano called Krakatoa and complete the exercise.

1 Where ....

2 When ....

3 Facts about the explosion:

  a ....

  b ....

  c ....

  d ....

  ....

  e ....

4 Results of the explosion:

  a ....

  b ....

  c ....

  ....

5 Examples of new life:

  a ....

  b ....

  c ....

  d ....

6 Listen to the tape again and then write questions for the following answers. Here is an example to show you:

                  Question   *Answer*

  a How many people were killed?   a 36,000

  b .... b 35 m

Unit 8 **Environment and ecology**

c .... c Java

d .... d Australia

e .... e 100 m

f .... f 24 hours

g .... g 28 Aug. 1883

h .... h 3 years

i .... i 1900

j .... j greenery

Section 2 **Weather**

Part A **Climate**

VOCABULARY
Scrub land (noun) ground covered with trees or bushes of poor quality
Debris (noun) scattered fragments of something which has been broken
Current (noun) (here) air moving in a given direction

Section 2 **Weather**

Precipitation (noun) (here) the fall of snow and rain
To shrink (verb) to get smaller
To soak up (verb) to absorb
To swell (verb) (here) to expand
To jeopardise (verb) to put in danger
To radiate (verb) to send out rays of light
To reflect (verb) (here) to throw back light (or heat)
CO_2 carbon dioxide
O_2 oxygen
SO_2 sulphur dioxide

A group of international experts in climatology are being interviewed on the radio about changing weather patterns around the world. Those taking part are Jenny Mason (BBC reporter), Pat Davenport (from Britain), Rod MacDougall (from the USA) and Lars Bengtsson (from Sweden).
Listen to the conversation about changing weather patterns around the world and fill in the details.

1 Increase in CO_2 is caused by

   a ....

   b ....
2 Variables affecting weather

   a ....

   b ....

   c ....

   d ....
3 Types of volcanoes

   a ....

   b ....
4 Rainfall patterns after volcanic eruptions

   a ....

   b ....

   c ....

Unit 8 **Environment and ecology**

5 Long-term effects

a ....

b ....

c ....

d ....

e ....

Listen to the tape again and choose the correct answer for each of the following. Put a circle around **a**, **b**, **c** or **d** to indicate your choice.

1 In the long term the weather will be
   a quite a bit warmer.
   b a bit warmer.
   c about the same temperature.
   d slightly cooler.

2 The amount of CO_2 in the atmosphere is increasing because
   a rain forests are being cut down.
   b more fossil fuels are being produced.
   c the Amazon River is flooding.
   d none of the above.

3 The polar ice caps
   a are responsible for the colder weather.
   b are increasing in size.
   c reflect the sunlight.
   d are changing position.

4 When Mt Etna erupts it can have
   a a serious effect on the weather.
   b an immediate effect on the weather.
   c a long-term effect on the weather.
   d none of the above.

5 The stratosphere has
   a a great many vertical currents.
   b only a few vertical currents.
   c no vertical currents.
   d extremely strong vertical currents.

Section 2 **Weather**

6 After an explosive eruption, the rainfall
  a increases considerably for several years.
  b increases only in the first few months.
  c increases after a year.
  d increases for about a year.

7 In future, agricultural areas will
  a be seriously affected by the weather.
  b tend to move southwards.
  c be richer and more irrigated.
  d have much more rainfall.

This exercise is about the volcanoes that are mentioned on the tape. Listen again to the part of the discussion about the volcanoes and fill in the table.

	Name, place	Date of eruption	Effects
1			
2		1815	
3		1980	
4			

79

Unit 8 **Environment and ecology**

Continue listening to the section of the discussion about the volcanoes. Identify the two different types of volcanoes on the diagrams and mark the stratosphere and troposphere.

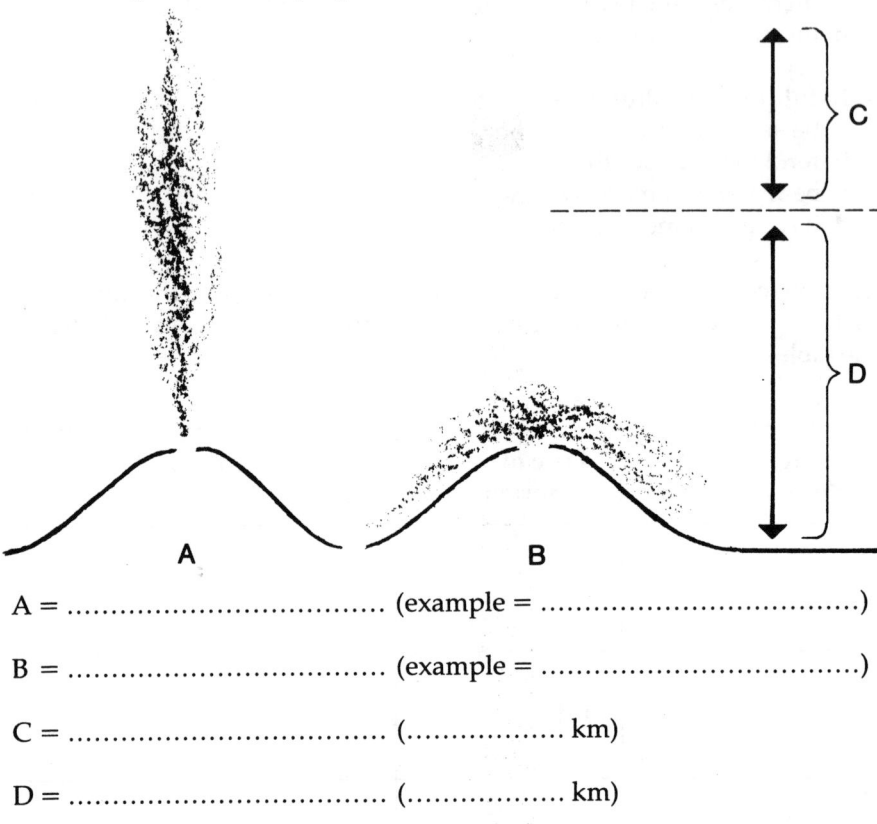

A = ... (example = ...)

B = ... (example = ...)

C = ... (................ km)

D = ... (................ km)

FOLLOW-UP
1 In pairs, ask your partner questions about the weather in his/her city, region or country. Find out about temperatures, rainfall, windy periods and the differences in the seasons and also about any unusual weather patterns.
2 Prepare a radio discussion programme where you can interview people who have been involved in unusual weather situations. Half the group can prepare questions and the other half can be the people involved. Here are some examples:

   a a sea captain near Krakatoa in August, 1883
   b a farmer who lives near Mt St Helens
   c a family who live near El Chichon
   d a climatologist from Indonesia
   e an Icelandic fisherman in May, 1783
   f a specialist in typhoons and hurricanes

Section 2 **Weather**

Part B **Forecast**

Listen to this weather summary at the end of a radio news programme. First there is a general summary of weather patterns around the world, and this is followed by precise conditions and temperatures.

Listen to the first part of the tape and complete this table.

Area/Country	Weather pattern
1	Cloudy
2 Europe	
3 Mediterranean	
4	
5 Canada	
6	
7	
8	Dry and warm
9	
10	

Unit 8 **Environment and ecology**

Listen to the second part of the weather report and complete this table. Use the letters to represent the conditions.

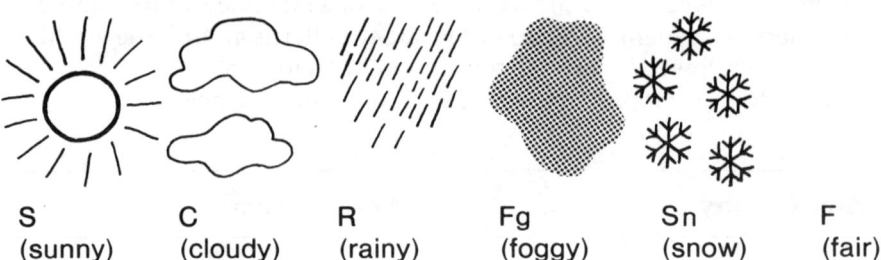

S	C	R	Fg	Sn	F
(sunny)	(cloudy)	(rainy)	(foggy)	(snow)	(fair)

City	Temperature (°C)	Conditions
1 Amsterdam	8	F
2		
3		
4		C
5 Moscow		
6		
7		
8	24	
9		
10		
11 Tokyo		
12		
13		
14		F
15		

Section 3 **Oil pollution**

VOCABULARY

Slick (noun) oil spilled on the surface of the water
Sludge (noun) thick dirty oil (or mud)
Dispersant (noun) something which scatters or breaks up something else, such as an oil spill
Absorbant (noun) something which takes in or soaks up something else, such as an oil spill
Hull (noun) the body or frame of a ship
Hinge (noun) a joint on which a door or lid swings
Core (noun) the central part
To mop up (verb) to clean up a spilled liquid
To suck (verb) (here) to draw up liquid through a pipe into a container
I'm all ears (idiomatic phrase) I'm listening attentively
You're pulling my leg (idiomatic phrase) you're making fun of me by telling me something untrue
Well, I never! (idiomatic phrase) I'm completely surprised
Whatever next! (idiomatic phrase) How amazing, I can't believe it. Whatever will happen next!

Two people are talking about new methods for dealing with oil pollution on the sea. David is British and Andy is from the United States. Listen to the conversation and pay special attention to the facts and figures about each of the five methods. Then fill in the table.

Unit 8 Environment and ecology

	Pillows	Hinged ship
a Size		35 m
b Description		
c Country	United States	
d Method		
e Advantages		

Section 3 **Oil pollution**

	Bacteria	Goblin	Dam atolls
a			
b		Catamaran-style ship	
c			
d			Oil drawn into core, in groups → keep oil until removal
e	Eaten by natural population, so no pollution		

Unit 8 **Environment and ecology**

FOLLOW-UP

There has been a tanker accident near your country and you are preparing a radio programme about it. Divide into two groups: one group will be reporters and journalists and the other group will be people involved in or affected by the accident. Prepare interviews with the following:

a the captain of the tanker
b a crew member who was injured
c the owner of the tanker
d the importer of the chicken-feather pillows
e a crew member from the hinged ship
f a specialist on oil-eating bacteria
g a pilot flying over the scene
h a representative from the Goblin company
i a government official from the Department of the Environment
j an oil company pollution expert
k a fisherman who saw the accident

Unit 9 **Personality**

Section 1 **Graphology**

VOCABULARY
Graphology (noun) the study of handwriting as a guide to character
To doodle (verb) to scribble or draw aimlessly while one's attention is engaged elsewhere
Trait (noun) distinguishing feature or characteristic
To procrastinate (verb) to defer or put off action until later
Angular (adj.) something with sharp or pointed corners
Tangled (adj.) intertwined or mixed up

American graphologist Denise Carpenter is being interviewed by radio reporter Leo Withers. Now listen to the tape and answer the questions.

1 What might just have been said by the interviewer before the tape begins which makes Denise Carpenter give this answer?

   ....

   ....

   ....

2 What started Denise's interest in graphology?

   ....

   ....

   ....

3 Why does Denise think that handwriting and doodling tell us about people's character?

   ....

   ....

   ....

4 Concerning Denise:
   a What does she do as a job now?

   ....

   b How long has she been doing it?

   ....

Unit 9 **Personality**

5 Give four personality traits which Denise says can be identified from handwriting.

a ....

b ....

c ....

d ....

6 In the table below are the kinds of letter *t* described by Denise. Beside each one fill in what she says it indicates about the character of the writer. They are not in the order described on the tape.

a		d	
b		e	
c		f	

7 In the story about Harry Benson, why was Denise's handwriting interpretation important?

....

....

....

8 How does Denise describe doodling?

....

....

....

Section 1 **Graphology**

9 In the table below are some of the doodles described in the interview. Beside each one write down what it tells about the character of the person who drew it.

a

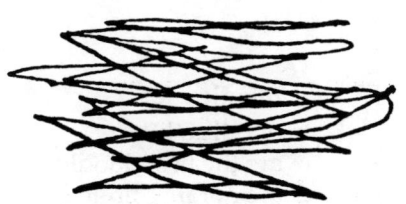

b

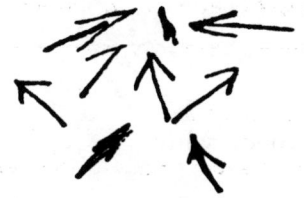

c

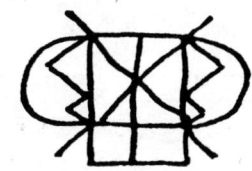

d

e

Unit 9 **Personality**

10 Using the information given on the tape, after each of the following statements choose **a, b, c** or **d** from the alternatives to complete the sentence.

  i Fashion designers

  ii Writers

  iii Architects

  iv Bank managers

  v Children

  vi People with disabilities

  a doodle a lot
  b doodle a little
  c are the best doodlers
  d are not mentioned

11 What does Denise say about people who doodle with:
  a ordinary pens?

  ....

  b pencils?

  ....

  c felt-tip pens?

  ....

FOLLOW-UP
Draw a few doodles of your own and then in groups or pairs try to decide what they mean.

Section 2 **Palmistry**

Part A **Interpreting hands**

VOCABULARY
Saturnine (adj.) gloomy, brooding
To taper (verb) to become gradually narrower at the end
Knotty (adj.) having lots of knots, lumps or bumps
Bigoted (adj.) intolerant, narrow-minded, thinking that one's own views are right
Cowardly (adj.) not brave, easily frightened
Philistine (adj.) uncultured, interested only in material things and proud to be so
Hedonistic (adj.) pleasure-seeking
Gullible (adj.) naive, easily deceived

Dr Henry Ryan is a psychologist and has recently been making a study of palmistry. You will hear an excerpt from his lecture; he gives some of his findings.
   Now listen to the tape and answer the questions.

1 What are the three kinds of hand interpretation which are mentioned in the talk concerned with
   a chiromancy?
   b chirognomy?
   c dermatoglyphics?

Unit 9 **Personality**

2 Use the letters A, B, C or D to mark on the diagram the four areas of the hand described by Dr Ryan and then in the table fill in what each one relates to.

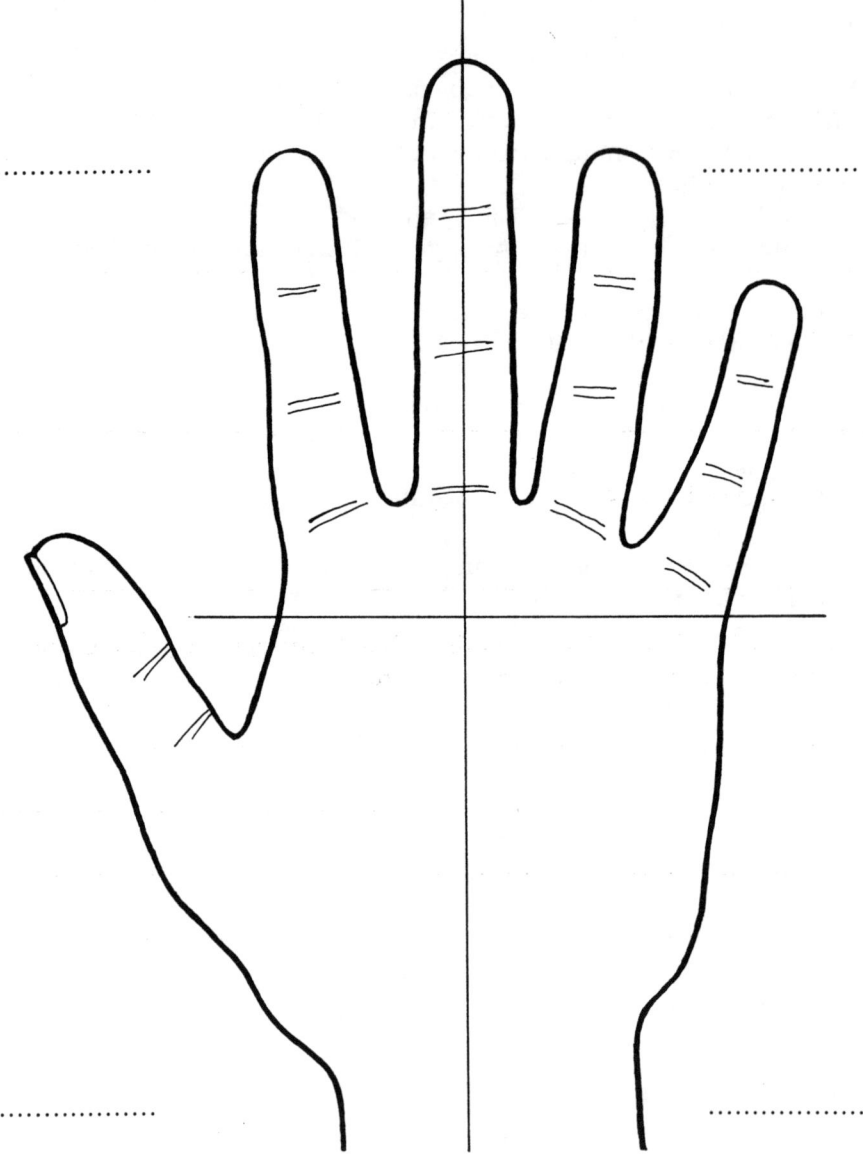

Section 2 **Palmistry**

Name of area	Relates to
a Inner active area	
b Outer active area	
c Inner passive area	
d Outer passive area	

3 Outline briefly why Dr Ryan thinks that there might be a connection between the hand and a person's character.

    ....

    ....

    ....

    ....

Unit 9 **Personality**

4 In the next table, the palmist's names for the different fingers are given. Fill in which finger the name refers to and what aspect of the character each one is supposed to reveal.

Name of finger	Finger indicated	Aspect of character revealed
a Finger of Jupiter		
b Finger of Saturn		
c Finger of Apollo		
d Finger of Mercury		

Section 2 **Palmistry**

5 Beside each of the five types of finger illustrated below (which are not in the order given on the tape) write the description of the finger given and the characteristics each one is supposed to indicate. One finger type has been done for you as an example.

Finger type	Characteristics
a	
b	
c Finger with smooth joints	
d	
e	

Unit 9 **Personality**

6 Fill in the names of the various mounts on the diagram of the hand given below. There is also a list of the names of the mounts (not in the order described by Dr Ryan) and one mount has already been marked for you.

Mount of Mercury
Mount of Jupiter
Mount of Venus
Mount of the Moon
Mount of Apollo
Mount of Saturn
Upper mount of Mars
Lower mount of Mars

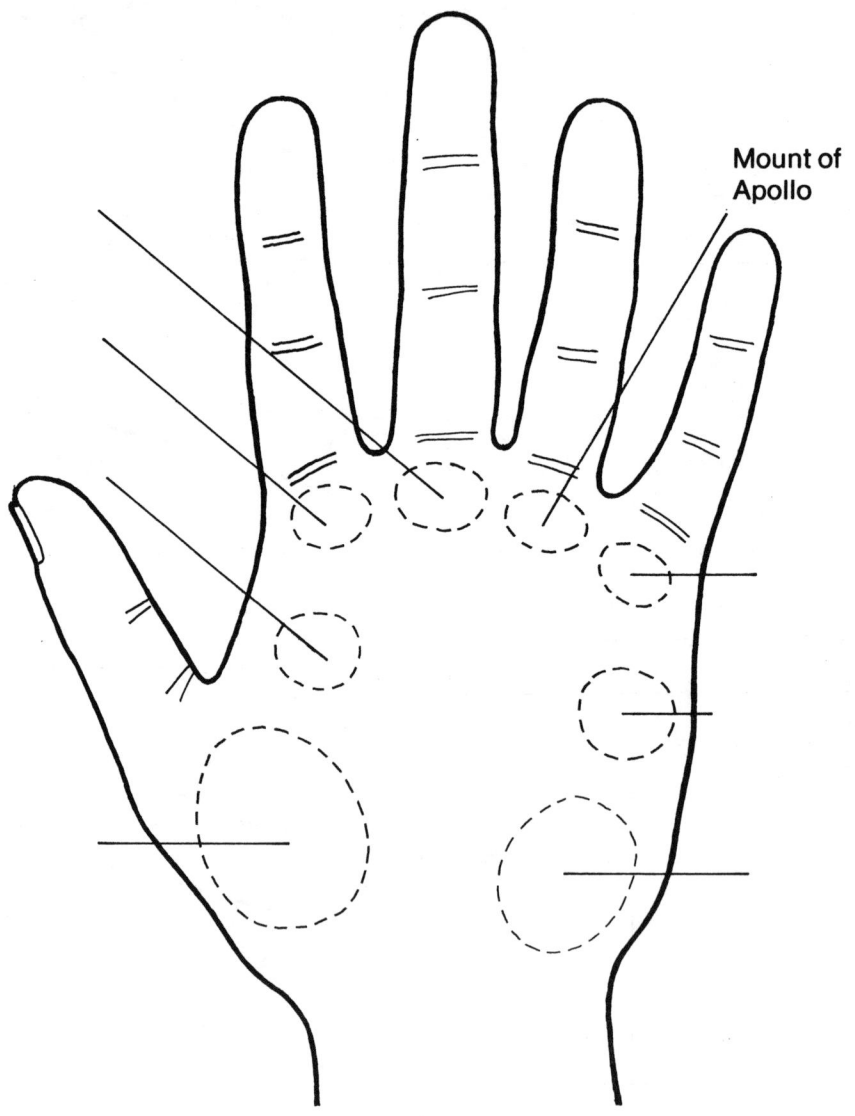

Section 2 **Palmistry**

7 Fill in the table below with the information given by Dr Ryan about the various bumps on the hand. Some have already been done for you as examples.

Name of mount	Character if it's flat	Character if it's normal	Character if it's large
a Mount of Venus		Healthy, warm-hearted, sincere	
b Mount of the Moon			
c Upper mount of Mars		Morally courageous	
d Lower mount of Mars			
e Mount of Jupiter			
f Mount of Saturn	Dullness		
g Mount of Apollo			
h Mount of Mercury			Good sense of humour

Unit 9 **Personality**

FOLLOW-UP
In pairs, study the various mounts on the palms of your hands. Using the information given, try to interpret each other's character.

Part B **Pronunciation**

Listen to the instructions on the tape and mark a tick [✓] or a cross [×] in the boxes, according to whether the *l* is pronounced or not. The key words in the sentences have been reproduced for you.

Example A could   [×]   (*l* not pronounced)
Example B milk   [✓]   (*l* pronounced)

1 half   [ ]   9 talk   [ ]
2 fold   [ ]   10 behalf [ ]
3 bulk   [ ]   11 silk   [ ]
4 walk   [ ]   12 salmon [ ]
5 folk   [ ]   13 yolks   [ ]
6 palm   [ ]   14 calm   [ ]
7 field   [ ]   15 told   [ ]
8 should   [ ]

Section 3 **Astrology**

VOCABULARY
Horoscope (noun) a set of astrological predictions of events in a person's life
Aquarius (noun) eleventh sign of the Zodiac, 21 January – 19 February
Gemini (noun) third sign of the Zodiac, 22 May – 21 June
Cancer (noun) fourth sign of the Zodiac, 22 June – 23 July
Overly (adv.) excessively
Libra (noun) seventh sign of the Zodiac, 24 September – 23 October
Aries (noun) first sign of the Zodiac, 21 March – 20 April
Taurus (noun) second sign of the Zodiac, 21 April – 21 May

This is a discussion between Jo and Simon who are talking about astrology. Jo is interested in astrology and has recently begun studying it seriously.
    Now listen to the tape and answer the questions. Put a circle around **a, b, c** or **d** to indicate your choice.

1 In which month could the discussion have been taking place?
   a In May.
   b In August.

98

Section 3 **Astrology**

    c In October.
    d In January.

2 Simon is amazed people believe in astrology because
    a what is predicted never happens to him.
    b it is written in newspapers and magazines.
    c he thinks that it is all nonsense.
    d one prediction cannot be true for lots of people.

3 Jo says that newspaper and magazine horoscopes
    a are too general to be as accurate as true astrology.
    b are only concerned with the planet Saturn.
    c have a bad effect on the reader.
    d are only pretending to give a prediction.

4 In astrology
    a the Sun sign you are born under is very important.
    b the ascendant sign is the most important factor.
    c the Sun sign is the one rising at the moment of your birth.
    d the Sun sign is completely irrelevant.

5 In an astrological chart
    a if you are born at 9 o'clock it will make you a Gemini ascendant.
    b the pattern changes eleven times every day.
    c the sun changes fifteen times every hour.
    d if you are born at 11.30 it will make you a Cancer ascendant.

6 When there are twins
    a one may be more aggressive than normal.
    b they will both have the same character.
    c one will probably have a different character from the other.
    d one will have a bad astrological aspect.

7 The ascendant tells about
    a your personality.
    b your potential.
    c your future.
    d your past.

8 If your ascendant is Libra, you are probably
    a musical.
    b orderly.
    c shy.
    d congenial.

Unit 9 **Personality**

9 If your sign is ruled by the planet Uranus, your character is
   a disturbed.
   b changeable.
   c indifferent.
   d unstable.

10 If your sign is Taurus, you have
   a an Air sign and you are beautiful.
   b an Earth sign and you are unstable.
   c an Air sign and like beauty.
   d an Earth sign and like security.

11 What will the sixth sign of the Zodiac be?
   a Earth.
   b Water.
   c Air.
   d Fire.

12 At the end of the discussion, Simon is
   a still very sceptical about astrology.
   b completely convinced about astrology.
   c showing greater interest in astrology.
   d asking Jo to do his chart just to please her.

FOLLOW-UP
In groups or pairs, discuss whether you think astrology has any bearing on the character, and also why you think it has persisted for so many thousands of years.

Unit 10 **Entertainment and leisure**

Section 1 **Home computers**

VOCABULARY

Software (noun) computer programs, the instructions for a computer
Hardware (noun) the computers and peripheral machines
Password (noun) the word that enables you to get at the information in a computer
To transmit data (verb) to send information
To break into a computer (verb) to gain access to the information in a computer
To spring up (verb) to begin suddenly
To fill a gap (idiomatic phrase) to remedy a deficiency
Time on your hands (idiomatic phrase) spare time
It's on the cards (idiomatic phrase) it's possible, likely
To be in store (idiomatic phrase) to be forthcoming, imminent

Listen to the talk by a computer expert about the changes and developments in the computer field and fill in the blanks.

1 The ISDN can transmit

   a ....

   b ....

   c ....

2 The recession led to a ....

                         b ....

   which in turn led to c ....

3 Successful new industries are

   a ....

   b ....

   c ....

Unit 10 **Entertainment and leisure**

4 The uses of PCs are

a ....

b ....

c ....

5 Interest in PCs

Age	Interest	Disapproval
a	%	%
b	%	%

6 Examples of fitness gadgets

a ....

b ....

7 Rubik's cube had

a .... sides

b .... faces each

c .... combinations

8 A hacker is ....

9 The essentials of hacking are

a ....

b ....

c ....

Section 1 **Home computers**

10 The problems involved with hacking are

   a ....

   b ....

Listen to the tape again and fill in the blanks. There is one word for each space. Here is an example to show you:

The world-wide telecommunications networks could transmit ..TELEX.

and ...VOICE... signals.

1 The increase in home computers is a result of the ....

2 Hundreds of companies have .... to fill the

   leisure-time ....

3 In the United States the second most important use of PCs was

   ....

4 Computer games have a .... life span.

5 A very light portable computer weighs under .... kg.

6 Fitness has become a real .... industry and it is prone to

   ....

7 There are watches to monitor your .... while

   you are .... or doing ....

8 Hackers can .... government or business

   computers by using the right ....

FOLLOW-UP
You are preparing a documentary radio programme about computers in the home. Based on the information on the tape and any personal experience, prepare interviews about PCs. Half the class can be the interviewers and prepare a list of questions, and the other half can

Unit 10 **Entertainment and leisure**

represent people with PCs and invent information. Here are some possible people to interview:

a a sociologist who specialises in redundancy problems
b the director of a centre for unemployed people
c the manager of a company which manufactures home computers
d a teenager with a home computer
e an opinion poll researcher who has just completed a study about PCs
f a pensioner who is interested in buying a PC
g a specialist who designs software for PCs

Section 2 **Arts review**

VOCABULARY

a *General*
Blockbuster (noun) (here) very forceful and popular film, book, TV story
Chimpanzee (noun) an ape
Rundown (noun) a brief review, summary
Far-fetched (adj.) improbable, unlikely
Soppy (colloquial adj.) sentimental, silly
To be conned (colloquial verb) to be defrauded, tricked
To be dying to do (idiomatic phrase) to be anxious, desperate to do
Wishy-washy (idiomatic phrase) lacking in substance, weak
Rock-bottom (idiomatic phrase) very low (prices)
Chock-a-block (idiomatic phrase) crammed together, overfull
To pay through the nose (idiomatic phrase) to pay a lot more than something is worth
To get sidetracked (idiomatic phrase) to deviate from the path or plan

b *Books, drama*
Writer (noun) the person who creates poetry, a book, a play
Plot (noun) the story, the action
Characters (noun) the people in the story
Setting (noun) where the action takes place
Sequel (noun) a novel that continues a previous story

c *Music*
Composer (noun) a person who writes music
Lyrics (noun) the words of a song
LP (noun) a long-play record
Single (noun) a record with one song per side

Section 2 **Arts review**

d *Art*
Artist (noun) a person who paints
Canvas (noun) cloth on which a painting is done
Landscape (noun) a painting of natural scenery
Portrait (noun) a painting of a person, especially the face
Sculptor (noun) a person who creates sculptures
Marble (noun) a hard rock used for sculptures
Bronze (noun) a copper alloy used for sculptures

Listen to the radio discussion programme called 'Arts Review'. Make notes about the four topics discussed and the different opinions that each critic has.

Now listen to the introduction again and match the people and their jobs. Draw a line to connect the person and the job. There are more jobs than people.

Name	*Job*
	journalist
Luke	manager
Rick	singer
Penny	artist
Rosie	broadcaster
Toby	agent
	director

(Luke → broadcaster)

Now listen again to the first topic that is discussed and answer the following. Circle **a**, **b**, **c** or **d** to indicate your choice.

1 *Rain on the Panes* was Corrie Clifton's
   a first novel.
   b best novel.
   c previous novel.
   d latest novel.

2 The plot is impossible according to
   a Rick but not Toby.
   b Rosie but not Penny.
   c Rick and Toby.
   d Rosie and Penny.

3 With reference to the setting,
   a Rosie
   b Toby
   c Rick
   d none of them
   thought it was suitable.

Unit 10 Entertainment and leisure

4 The characterisation was one of the worst features according to
   a all of them.
   b Toby but not Rick.
   c Penny but not Rosie.
   d none of them.

5 a Rosie but not Penny
   b Toby and Rick
   c Penny but not Rick
   d None of them
   preferred the plot to the characters and setting.

Now listen again to the second topic and answer the following:

6 The film was about treasure which
   a had been lost in times of war.
   b was at the bottom of the sea.
   c was lost in violent circumstances.
   d was the result of shipwrecks.

7 a All of them
   b All but Rick
   c Only Penny and Toby
   d Only Luke
   agreed that it was good family entertainment.

8 The music was one of the least attractive parts of the film according to
   a Rosie and Toby.
   b Rosie and Rick.
   c all of them.
   d Rosie.

9 The plot was appreciated by
   a all of them.
   b all but Rick.
   c only Rick.
   d only Penny and Toby.

10 Toby enjoyed the film so much that he
   a saw it again the next day.
   b told all his friends to see it.
   c took Rosie to see it again.
   d stayed at the cinema to see it a second time.

Section 2 **Arts review**

Now listen again to the third topic and answer the following:

11 The name of the pop group is
   a Dead-Eye Dick and the Depressed Den.
   b Dead-Eye Dan and the Depressed Den.
   c Dead-Eye Dick and the Grim Den.
   d Dead-Eye Dan and the Grim Den.

12 Rosie is
   a middle-aged.
   b thirty.
   c too old for pop music.
   d older than thirty.

13 Toby listened to the album because
   a he wanted to.
   b he had to.
   c he likes pop music.
   d Rick recommended it.

14 Penny
   a liked this record.
   b didn't like this record.
   c didn't comment on it.
   d didn't listen to it.

15 Rick thinks that
   a only young people
   b mainly young people
   c anybody
   d mainly old people
   can get depressed.

Now listen again to the fourth topic and answer the following:

16 The exhibition featured work done by
   a people under forty.
   b animals.
   c people around fifty.
   d all of the above.

Unit 10 **Entertainment and leisure**

17 Rick
    a enjoyed the exhibition but didn't make any comments.
    b didn't see the exhibition but made some comments.
    c didn't enjoy the exhibition.
    d agreed with Penny's comments about this exhibition.

18 The exhibition was
    a mainly paintings, with a few sculptures.
    b both paintings and sculptures.
    c mainly landscape paintings.
    d only pop art.

19 a Only Rick
    b All of them
    c Rick and Rosie
    d None of them
    thought that some of today's modern art is a waste of money.

20 The sculptures were particularly appreciated by
    a both Penny and Toby.
    b Toby.
    c all of them.
    d Rosie.

Now listen again to the preview of next week's programme and answer the True/False statements. Mark T for True and F for False. Here is an example:

Next week's programme is at the same time.	T

1 The concert features mainly Beethoven.	
2 The exhibition is at the Symphony Hall.	
3 The opera *Flora Fidelis* is new.	
4 The TV programme is about astronomy.	
5 The opera is coming from Paris.	

Section 2 **Arts review**

FOLLOW-UP

The class is divided into four groups. Each group will choose one of the following and discuss it. Then one person from each group will present the views to the rest of the class.

a a new bestseller
b a recent film
c a popular record or pop group
d a well-known TV programme
e a recent concert or opera
f an exhibition at a gallery or museum

Unit 10 **Entertainment and leisure**

Section 3 **Programme news**

Part A **Radio programmes**

Radio announcers are giving details and information about forthcoming programmes. Listen to the tape and fill in the table on the opposite page. Some have already been done for you.

Part B **Pronunciation**

Listen to the instructions on the tape and mark a 1 or 2 in the spaces below, according to whether the stress is on the first syllable [1] or the second syllable [2]. The key words in the sentences have been reproduced for you.

Example A récords   [1]
Example B recórded   [2]

1 present   [1]
2 suspect   [   ]
3 imports   [   ]
4 conducting   [   ]
5 conflict   [   ]
6 permitted   [   ]
7 object   [   ]
8 projected   [   ]
9 converted   [   ]
10 surveyed   [   ]
11 progress   [   ]
12 produced   [   ]

Section 3 **Programme news**

Radio channel	Day and time	Name	Description
1			
2		Six O'Clock News	
3 Radio 3			
4	8.50 p.m. Monday	Postbag	
5			
6			
7			Exciting thriller
8 Radio 2			
9			
10			
11			
12		Watchout	

Penguin Books
Penguin Skills Series

Penguin Listening Skills
Student's Book

Student's Book

Penguin Listening Skills

Stephen Kirby
Patty Key

Penguin Books

PENGUIN BOOKS

Published by the Penguin Group
27 Wrights Lane, London W8 5TZ, England
Viking Penguin Inc., 40 West 23rd Street, New York, New York 10010, USA
Penguin Books Australia Ltd, Ringwood, Victoria, Australia
Penguin Books Canada Ltd, 2801 John Street, Markham, Ontario, Canada L3R 1B4
Penguin Books (NZ) Ltd, 182–190 Wairau Road, Auckland 10, New Zealand

Penguin Books Ltd, Registered Offices: Harmondsworth, Middlesex, England

First published 1985
10 9 8 7 6 5 4 3 2

Copyright © Stephen Kirby and Patty Key, 1985
All rights reserved

Reproduced, printed and bound in Great Britain by
Hazell Watson & Viney Limited
Member of BPCC plc
Aylesbury, Bucks, England

Set in VIP Palatino and Helvetica by Wyvern Typesetting Ltd, Bristol

Except in the United States of America, this book is sold subject
to the condition that it shall not, by way of trade or otherwise, be lent,
re-sold, hired out, or otherwise circulated without the
publisher's prior consent in any form of binding or cover other than
that in which it is published and without a similar condition
including this condition being imposed on the subsequent purchaser

Contents

Introduction 7

Unit 1 **Health**
Section 1 **Colds** 9
  Part A Medicine 9
  Part B Directions 10
  Part C Folk cures 11
Section 2 **Fitness** 12
  Part A Training programmes 12
  Part B A fitness timetable 14
Section 3 **Old age** 16

Unit 2 **Places and people**
Section 1 **China** 20
  Part A Census 20
  Part B Conference delegates 21
Section 2 **Tourists in Japan** 22
  Part A Tourist office 22
  Part B Factory tour 24
Section 3 **Quiz** 25

Unit 3 **Crime and the law**
Section 1 **Witnesses** 30
Section 2 **Court case** 32
Section 3 **Burglaries** 34

Unit 4 **Jobs**
Section 1 **Getting a job** 37
Section 2 **Interviews** 39
Section 3 **Phone-in** 42

Unit 5 **Sport**
Section 1 **Round-up** 46
Section 2 **Olympics** 49
Section 3 **Sport in Britain** 53

Unit 6 **Technology**
Section 1 **Cross-Channel power** 55
  Part A The project 55
  Part B Tag questions 58
Section 2 **Tiny TVs** 58
Section 3 **Hot off the press** 61

Contents

Unit 7 Fashion
Section 1 **Psychology of clothes** — 64
Section 2 **Fashion model** — 66
Section 3 **Fashion notebook** — 69

Unit 8 Environment and ecology
Section 1 **Volcanoes** — 72
　Part A Mt Etna — 72
　Part B Krakatoa — 74
Section 2 **Weather** — 76
　Part A Climate — 76
　Part B Forecast — 81
Section 3 **Oil pollution** — 83

Unit 9 Personality
Section 1 **Graphology** — 87
Section 2 **Palmistry** — 91
　Part A Interpreting hands — 91
　Part B Pronunciation — 98
Section 3 **Astrology** — 98

Unit 10 Entertainment and leisure
Section 1 **Home computers** — 101
Section 2 **Arts review** — 104
Section 3 **Programme news** — 110
　Part A Radio programmes — 110
　Part B Pronunciation — 110

Introduction

By the time you use this book you will be a student who already has a good knowledge of English and who can generally understand it. There may, however, be times when you need to be able to do more than just comprehend what is being said – for instance, when you need to make notes on what you are listening to or when you come into a conversation half-way through and want to pick up the general idea of what is being discussed.

In your professional and personal life there will be situations where you will hear and have to absorb a lot of details, facts and figures and then extract some points from them. In your private life you may wish to listen to talks in English about subjects you are interested in. You may also be a full-time student of English who now wishes to consolidate what you have learnt in order to progress to other and more difficult areas. The aims of this book are to satisfy all these needs and many more besides.

Listening does not exist in a vacuum but is only one part of the communication process. Clearly, it would not be possible to allow for immediate spoken replies to the questions in this book. However, to give you the chance to practise what you have learnt in the way of vocabulary and terminology, most sections have follow-up exercises which will give you the chance to use your newly-acquired language at once. It is hoped that all the topics will be useful for you and provide variety and interest in a whole range of different areas.

We should, finally, explain that the tapescripts are not authentically recorded, for various reasons. Apart from the obvious difficulty of poor recording and sound reproduction, a major point to consider is that any listener who is concentrating on what is being said tends to 'switch off' background sounds and pay attention to what is being addressed to him/her. Distracting noises are not usually what impairs the ability to comprehend but this is usually due to a failure to understand what is being said. For this reason the tapescripts are 'semi-authentic' in that they are exactly what would be said in the situations covered in the book. They are in the style of natural spoken English with all the necessary lubricants, hesitations and other similar idiosyncrasies of speech, but they are free from unnecessary distractions.

We hope you will have as much pleasure in using this book as we have had in preparing it.

Stephen Kirby
Patty Key

Folkestone, 1984

Unit 1 **Health**

Section 1 **Colds**

Part A **Medicine**

VOCABULARY

To tell the truth (idiomatic phrase) to say exactly what you feel; to give an honest opinion
Bless you (idiomatic phrase) what you say after someone sneezes
By the way (idiomatic phrase) what you say when you suddenly remember something or you want to add a comment
To be off (verb) to leave

Now listen to the conversation between Daniel, a Spanish student, and Kira from Greece. They are studying in England and Kira is asking about medicines for a cold. From the description on the tape choose the correct bottle and put a circle around A, B, C or D to indicate your choice.

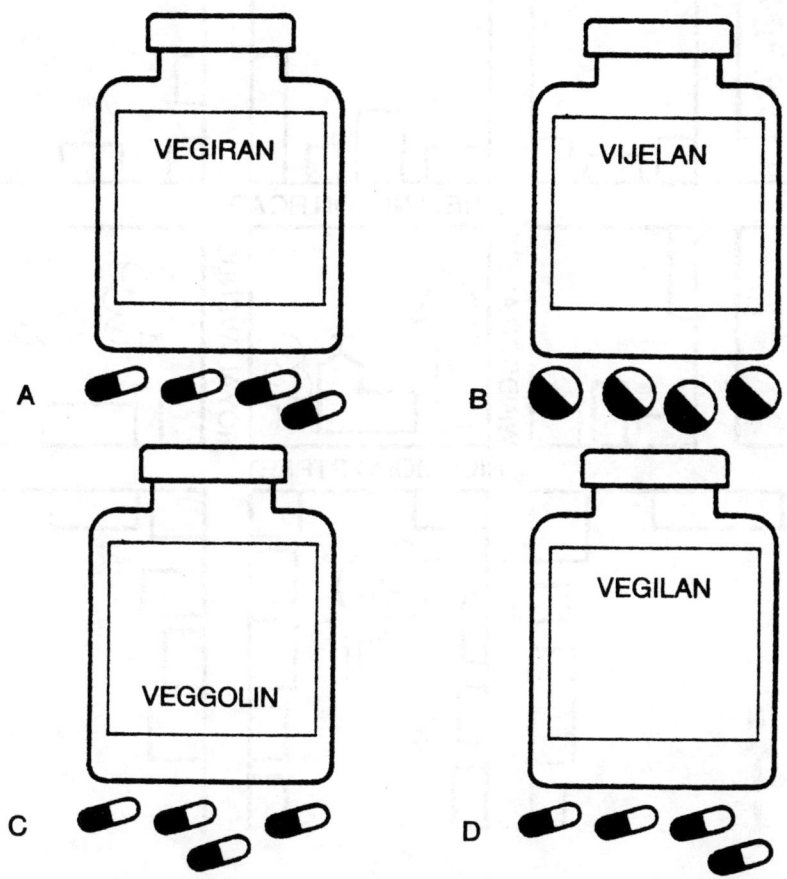

Unit 1 **Health**

Part B **Directions**

Listen to the directions and mark the route to the chemist's using arrows, like this:

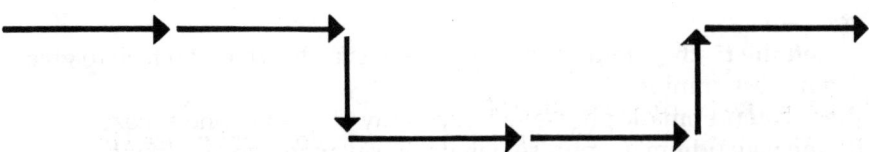

Then mark the following places on the map using these letters:
  Greengrocer's: G
  Chemist's: C
  Shoe shop: S
  Bank: B

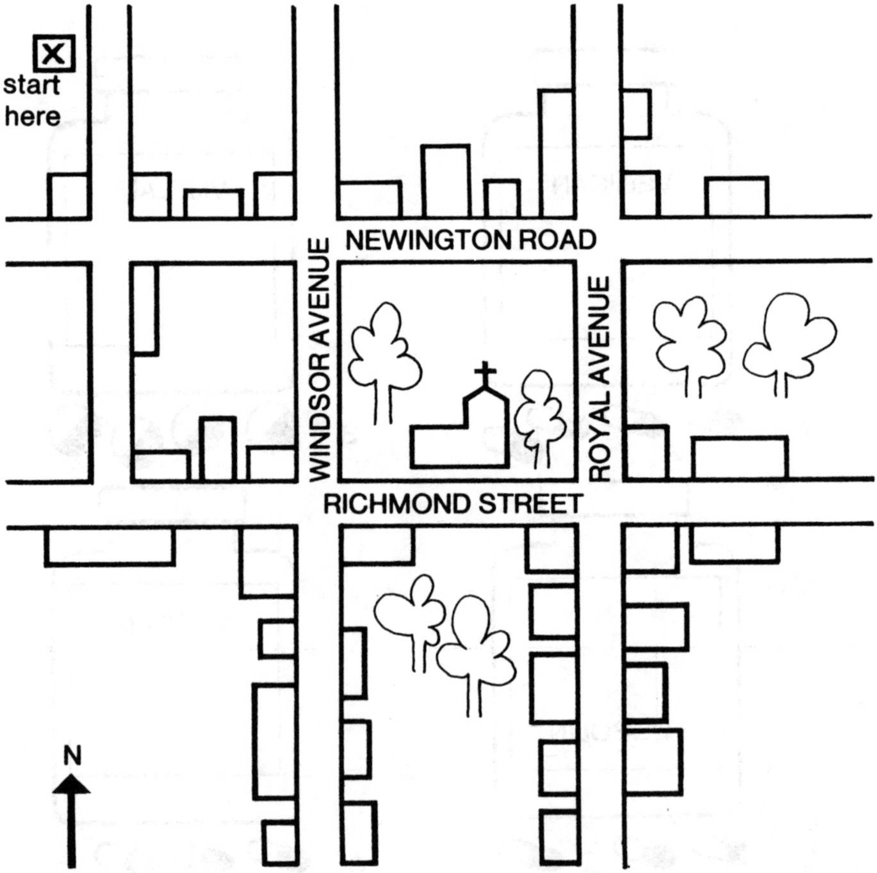

Section 1 **Colds**

Part C **Folk cures**

VOCABULARY
To cure (verb) to make better, to improve
To sweat (verb) to perspire
To infect (verb) to fill someone with germs or a disease
Smashing (adj., colloquial) wonderful, lovely
To have a go (verb, colloquial) to try
Garlic (noun) a small bulb, a member of the onion family, used in cooking
Nettle (noun) a wild plant with leaves which sting if touched
Licorice (noun) a plant used in making medicines or sweets
Herring (noun) a type of fish, often pickled or smoked
Yak (noun) a large cow-like animal found in the Himalayas

Kira is talking to an old man in the chemist's about different methods for curing colds. Listen to the conversation and fill in the table.

Country/Group	Cure
1 England	
2	
3	Dried herrings
4 Gypsies	
5	

FOLLOW-UP
In pairs or small groups discuss different cold remedies you are familiar with or have heard about. Then present your findings to the others.

Unit 1 **Health**

Section 2 **Fitness**

Part A **Training programmes**

VOCABULARY
To get the ball rolling (idiomatic phrase) to begin, to start
Rigorous (adj.) severe, harsh
Frugal (adj.) economical, costing little
The latest craze (idiomatic phrase) the most recent trend or fashion
Compulsory (adj.) obligatory

	West Germany
a Where	
b How long	
c Who	
d Exercises	
e Lectures, discussions	
f Benefits, advantages	

Section 2 **Fitness**

Voluntary (adj.) optional, up to the individual
To be keen on doing something to be enthusiastic, very interested
To pay in full to pay the whole amount
Outlook (noun) way of looking at something
Rejuvenated (adj.) feeling young again

Listen to the discussion about the health and fitness of employees. Maria is from Germany, Shigeru is Japanese and Mike comes from the United States. Fill in the details in the table.

USA	Japan

13

Unit 1 **Health**

Part B **A fitness timetable**

Notice the expressions using the verb *sound* followed by an adjective to express different emotions, for example surprise, agreement, anger, disgust and so on.

   That sounds terrible!
   Sounds good.
   It may sound crazy but . . .

Now listen to the sentences about the different fitness programmes and give a suitable reply using *sound* plus a suitable adjective. There are two examples on the tape, followed by six sentences.

FOLLOW-UP

In pairs or small groups plan a suitable fitness programme either for a weekend or for three days for a group of employees from:

a a car factory
b a bank
c a school
d an insurance company
e a hospital
f an airline

Present your programme to the others, who can make notes of the times and activities.

Section 2 **Fitness**

Here is a timetable to help with your programme.

Day →			
Morning	0600		
Afternoon	1400		
Evening	2000		

Unit 1 **Health**

Section 3 **Old age**

VOCABULARY

Geriatrics (noun) the diagnosis and treatment of diseases affecting old people
Gerontology (noun) the study of ageing and the problems associated with elderly people
To prolong (verb) to lengthen, to make longer
Life span (noun) length of life
Longevity (noun) long life
Bachelor (noun) a man who is not married
Spinster (noun) a woman who is not married
To hit the nail on the head (idiomatic phrase) to have the correct answer, to be exactly right
To reach a ripe old age (idiomatic phrase) to live a long time
Nomad (noun) a wanderer, a person moving from place to place
Spartan (adj.) simple, frugal, austere
To thrive (verb) to prosper, to flourish
Local (noun) your regular pub or bar
Incentive (noun) motive, reason

Listen to the conversation which takes place at an International Conference on Gerontology in Geneva, Switzerland. Six doctors, all specialists in geriatrics, are chatting after one of the sessions. They are: Dr Al Mofleh (Saudi Arabia), Dr Bandini (Italy), Dr Hernandez (Mexico), Dr Panapova (USSR), Dr Taylor (Great Britain) and Dr Whitman (Canada).

Section 3 **Old age**

Fill in the details of the old people on the table.

Age	Country/Group	Habits
1 95		
2	Japan	
3		
4		Spaghetti, olive oil, wine Interested in village life Walked everywhere
5		
6	Britain	
7		

17

Unit 1 **Health**

Now listen to the discussion again and choose the correct answer to the following questions. Put a circle around **a, b, c** or **d** to indicate your choice.

1 The old man from Canada
   a was disgusted with peanuts.
   b claimed that peanuts prolonged his life.
   c thought that peanuts would keep him fit.
   d ate 5 kg of peanuts a week.

2 The Canadian man smoked
   a rarely.
   b sometimes.
   c a pack a day.
   d heavily.

3 The man in Japan
   a had been married when he was young.
   b had never been married.
   c got married after he retired.
   d wanted to get married.

4 The Japanese man drank
   a rarely.
   b sometimes.
   c a bottle a day.
   d heavily.

5 The old people in the USSR
   a never live past 100.
   b do not enjoy life after 100.
   c die in their nineties.
   d are still living in their nineties.

6 In the USSR the people eat
   a a lot of yogurt, cheese and milk.
   b mainly meat and vegetables.
   c a bit of meat and a lot of yogurt.
   d plenty of fruit and vegetables and a little meat.

7 The sisters in Italy had spaghetti
   a once a day after the wine.
   b twice a day before the wine.
   c once a day before the wine.
   d twice a day with wine.

Section 3 **Old age**

8 The life style of the Italian women was similar to
  a the nomads.
  b the people in the USSR.
  c the man in Britain.
  d the lady in the United States.

9 The nomads live
  a in the desert.
  b all over Africa.
  c only in hot countries.
  d in small towns.

10 The nomads ate
  a a lot of meat but only a little fruit.
  b a lot of bread but only a little meat.
  c only fruit and vegetables.
  d a bit of fruit and vegetables.

11 The British man smoked
  a rarely.
  b only in the pub.
  c a lot.
  d sometimes.

12 The American woman lives with
  a her husband.
  b a friend.
  c her pets.
  d a maid.

FOLLOW-UP

1 In small groups, discuss the problems of old people in your community and try to decide what could be done to help them by:
  a the local council
  b volunteer groups
  c the national government

2 You are visiting a special home for old people where everyone is over a hundred years old. In pairs you interview these old people and pay special attention to facts about diet, exercise, interests, hobbies, activities and so on. Present the findings of each interview and try to draw conclusions about the old people's longevity.

Unit 2 **Places and people**

Section 1 **China**

Part A **Census**

Listen to the World Service report about the census in China and fill in the blanks. The information is not all in the same order as on the tape.

1 Census   **a** most recent ....

        b previous ....

2 Total population ....

3 Questionnaire   **a** number of questions ....

        b examples   **i** ....

          ii ....

          iii ....

        c number of computers ....

4 Increase since previous census = ... million

        = **a** $2\frac{1}{2}$ times ....

        b .... times ....

5 Percentage of men ....

6 Number in countryside ....

7 Number in armed forces ....

8 Population growth   **a** in 1964 .... %

        b in 1982 .... %

9 Birth rate   **a** hourly ....

        b daily ....

        c yearly ....

Section 1 **China**

FOLLOW-UP

1 Working in pairs or small groups, prepare a list of ten to fifteen questions suitable for a census.

2 In pairs, interview the following people for a census. One person will be the interviewer and ask the questions and the other will be one of the following characters:

a the mayor of the town/city
b a farmer
c a banker
d a housewife
e a football player
f a musician
g a film star
h a student
i a teacher
j a factory worker
k a pensioner

Part B **Conference delegates**

Four people of different nationalities at the United Nations Conference on World Population are sitting at a small table in a hotel lounge in Peking. Listen to the tape and make careful notes about the four delegates. For each one there is information about his country, his name and the colour of his tie. Then work out the solution and mark the answers on the diagram.

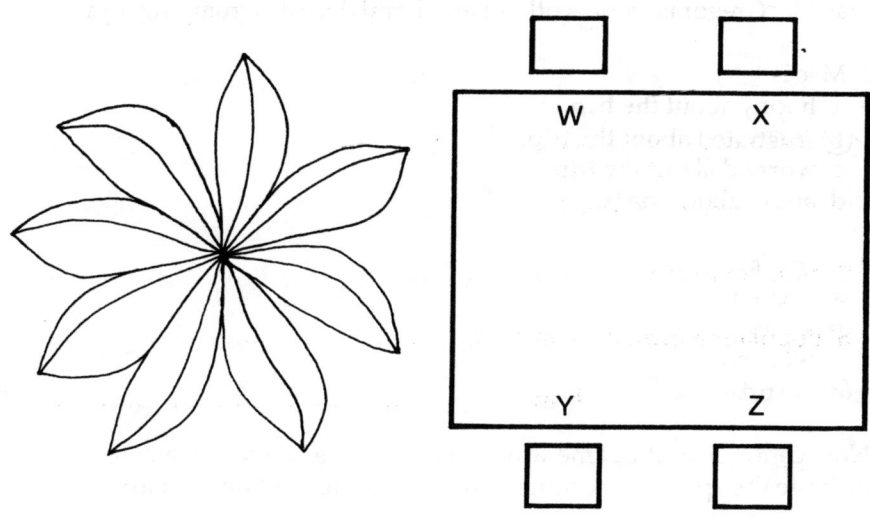

Unit 2 **Places and people**

Section 2 **Tourists in Japan**

Part A **Tourist office**

VOCABULARY
To be fed up with something (idiomatic phrase) to be tired, to have had enough
Bunch (noun) group, collection
Shop floor (noun) the production area in a factory
To snoop (verb) to sneak around, to look into matters that do not concern you
To spy (verb) to watch the movements of others and report them
To catch the drift (idiomatic phrase) to get the gist, to get the general idea

Two British businessmen in Japan go to a tourist office in Tokyo. They are talking to the manager about special tours of factories. Listen to the conversation and pay special attention to the intonation patterns of the businessmen. Are they angry, happy, disappointed, surprised and so on? When you have listened and thought about the intonation, then listen to the examples on the tape and choose the correct interpretation. Circle **a**, **b**, **c** or **d** to indicate your choice. The first two have been done for you as examples, and the answers are on the tape.

Mac MacGregor is from Scotland and Frank Floyd is from England.

1 Mac is
  a happy about the trip.
  (b) frustrated about the trip.
  c worried about the trip.
  d angry about the trip.

2 Frank is
  a excited.
  b angry.
  c worried.
  (d) surprised.

Now continue in the same way and choose the correct answer to indicate the speaker's feelings. The answers are not on the tape.

3 Mac is
  a angry with Frank.
  b trying to persuade Frank.

Section 2 **Tourists in Japan**

   c happy to be right.
   d worried about Frank.

4 Frank is
   a enthusiastic.
   b suspicious.
   c surprised.
   d angry.

5 Frank is
   a worried about it.
   b surprised about it.
   c suspicious.
   d not interested.

6 Mac is
   a impatient with Frank.
   b angry with Frank.
   c worried about Frank.
   d surprised at Frank.

7 Frank is
   a excited about it.
   b worried about it.
   c not interested.
   d suspicious.

8 Mac is
   a surprised.
   b condescending.
   c angry.
   d uncertain.

9 Frank is
   a unsure.
   b angry.
   c suspicious.
   d excited.

10 Frank is
   a amused.
   b worried.
   c angry.
   d inattentive.

Unit 2 **Places and people**

Part B **Factory tour**

Listen to the conversation and make notes in the table of the times and the factories mentioned.

1 Available tours

Time	Factories		
a 0830			
b	Nissan		
c 1130			
d		LUNCH	
e		Computers	
f		Hawasaki steelworks	

2 Mac and Frank's tours

Time	Factories
a	
b	
c	

Section 3 **Quiz**

FOLLOW-UP

1 In small groups, plan a one-day tour of your city, town or region that would be interesting for a group of:

　a students　　　　**e** factory workers
　b businessmen　　**f** engineers
　c housewives　　 **g** historians
　d pensioners　　 **h** teachers

2 In pairs, prepare dialogues at a travel agent's to arrange these tours. Use timetable 1 on page 24 as a guide. One person is the travel agent and the other is a representative of the group.

Section 3 **Quiz**

VOCABULARY

Contestant (noun) someone taking part in a competition
Free-for-all (noun) a discussion when everyone expresses his/her own view
Cliff-hanger (noun) something exciting that keeps you guessing until the very end
Home stretch (noun) the final part of a competition or game
Waltz (noun) ballroom dance with music in 3/4 time
To confer (verb) to discuss, to consult
To come up with (verb) to provide, to supply
To pip someone at the post (idiomatic phrase) to win narrowly at the very last second

1 Two schools are competing in a quiz about nationalities and geography. Listen to the introduction and mark first names and nationalities of the contestants and the teams on the plan.

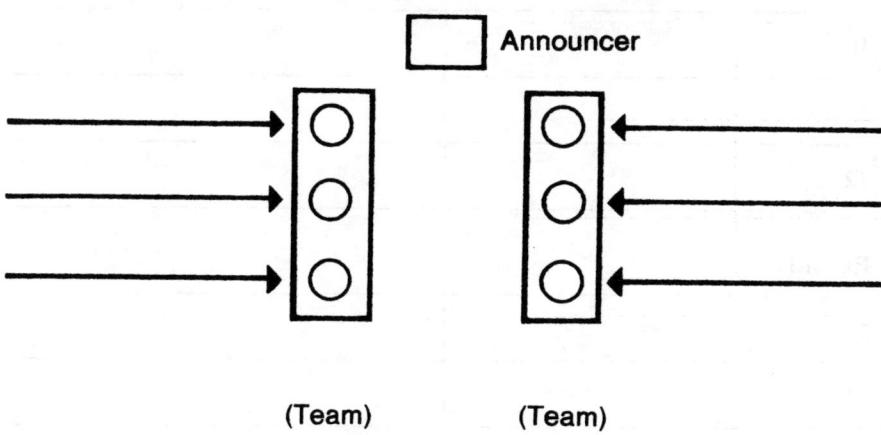

Unit 2 **Places and people**

2 Listen to the quiz and try to answer the questions yourself at the same time as the contestants. There are four rounds, with six questions in each round. Write your answer in the first column and the correct answer in the second column. The announcer will give the correct answer.

	Your answer	Correct answer
Round 1		
1		Mount Everest
2		
3		
4		
5		
6		
Round 2		
7		
8		
9		
10		
11		
12		
Round 3		
13		
14		

Section 3 **Quiz**

	Your answer	Correct answer
15		
16		
17		
18		

Round 4

19		
20		
21		
22		
23		
24		

3 Listen to the quiz again and answer the following True/False sentences for each round. Mark T for True or F for False. Here is an example:

The announcer's name is Fred.	F

Round 1

a There is no conferring in this round.	
b Maggie gives the correct answer for question 3.	
c Stan answers question 4 correctly.	
d Chelsea's captain gives the right answer for question 5.	

Unit 2 **Places and people**

e Barbara gets 1 point for question 6.	
f The score is a tie at the end of the round.	

Round 2

a The questions must be answered alternately by the teams.	
b The Belgrave captain answers question 7.	
c Deborah gets 1 point for question 10.	
d Barbara answers her question correctly.	
e Claudio gets 2 points for question 12.	
f Chelsea is ahead at the end of this round.	

Round 3

a Conferring is allowed in this round.	
b The questions must be answered alternately by the teams.	
c Chelsea answers question 14 correctly.	
d Belgrave is ahead after question 15.	
e Barbara gets 1 point for question 17.	
f Chelsea is ahead at the end of the round.	

Round 4

a Belgrave answers first in this round.	
b Stan answers question 19 correctly.	
c Deborah answers her question correctly.	

Section 3 **Quiz**

d Barbara answers her question correctly.	
e Chris gets 2 points for question 24.	
f The last round is a tie.	

FOLLOW-UP
In small groups plan a quiz programme based on

a geography
b history
c famous books, films, TV programmes, music
d sports

Write ten to fifteen questions for each section. Then divide the class into teams and, with an announcer, have a quiz.

Unit 3 **Crime and the law**

Section 1 **Witnesses**

VOCABULARY
Incident (noun) event
All of a sudden (adv. phrase) suddenly
To tug (verb) to pull
Thirtyish (adj.) about thirty
To stumble (verb) to trip or fall
Commotion (noun) noise or disturbance
To shove (verb) to push
Longish (adj.) fairly long

A policeman is interviewing three witnesses who have just seen a man steal a handbag from an elderly lady.
  Listen to the tape and fill in the notes in the policeman's notebook. Some information has been filled in already.

Time of robbery	11.45 a.m.
Place	High Street, in front of the supermarket
Name of witness	Mrs Jennifer Daniels
Address	
Position of witness	
Description of robber	
Description of incident	

Section 1 **Witnesses**

Name of witness

Address

Position of witness

Description of robber

Description of incident

Name of witness

Address

Position of witness

Description of robber

Description of incident

FOLLOW-UP

A group of two or three students should be ready to act out a crime, one as victim, the others as criminals. The remainder of the class should form two groups, one as 'witnesses', the other as 'police'. The 'police' go out of the room while the 'criminals' act out the crime in front of the 'witnesses', who watch from different parts of the room. The 'police' can then interview the 'witnesses' and make notes about the crime, which can be compared afterwards.

Unit 3 **Crime and the law**

Section 2 **Court case**

VOCABULARY

Magistrate (noun) a civil judge, usually a prominent member of the public
Offence (noun) a crime
Driving test (noun) examination which has to be taken in Britain to obtain a driving licence
Provisional licence (noun) the licence granted to people who are still learning to drive a motor vehicle
Cogent (adj.) forcible or compelling
To charge with (verb) to accuse somebody of committing a crime
To acquit (verb) to declare a person not guilty of a crime
Prosecution (noun) lawyer in Britain conducting a case in court against an accused person

Jill Knight is a radio interviewer who is talking to a former magistrate, Peter Walters, about his work.
  Listen to the interview and choose the correct answers to questions 1 to 6 by circling **a**, **b**, **c** or **d**.

1 Peter Walters found it hard
  a to decide whether offenders were guilty or not.
  b to give punishments that were hard enough.
  c to decide on a hard punishment for an offender.
  d to decide how to punish an offender.

2 In the case described by Peter Walters
  a a young man drove a car alone before passing his driving test.
  b a young man wasn't able to drive a car.
  c a young man couldn't drive a car before he was nineteen.
  d a young man couldn't drive a car the week before his test.

3 John's mother
  a had gone abroad with his father.
  b had gone to visit his sister who was ill.
  c had gone to visit her sister.
  d had gone to visit her aunt who was ill.

4 John
  a was stopped by the police because he hadn't got a licence.
  b desperately tried to remember where the house was.
  c was stopped by the police because he was exceeding the speed limit.
  d couldn't get a taxi for at least an hour.